Dear Parents:

Children learn to read in stages, and all children develop reading skills at different ages. **Ready Readers**™ were created to promote children's interest in reading and to increase their reading skills. **Ready Readers**™ are written on two levels to accommodate children ranging in age from three through eight. These stages are meant to be used only as a guide.

Stage 1: Preschool-Grade 1
Stage 1 books are written in very short, simple sentences with large type. They are perfect for children who are getting ready to read or are just becoming familiar with reading on their own.

Stage 2: Grades 1-3
Stage 2 books have longer sentences and are a bit more complex. They are suitable for children who are able to read but still may need help.

All the **Ready Readers**™ tell varied, easy-to-follow stories and are colorfully illustrated. Reading will be fun, and soon your child will not only be ready, but eager to read.

WHEN THE BLUEBIRD SINGS

Written by Donna Taylor
Illustrated by Edward Heck

Modern Publishing
A Division of Unisystems, Inc.
New York, New York 10022

I wake up
in the morning
when the bluebird sings.

"Good morning," I say to the big brown squirrel.

I brush my teeth.

I get dressed.

I eat my breakfast.

I go out to play.

I fly my airplane

and play ball.

Soon it's time for lunch!

What a big sandwich!

Gramps takes me to the store
in the afternoon.

I pay the cashier all by myself.

Gramps reads me a story,
while the red bird listens
in the afternoon.

Before I know it,
it's time for dinner,
a bath, and time to brush my
teeth again!

I get into bed...

...and fall asleep...

...until morning,
when the bluebird sings.